Magic Grandad's E Big Book of History: Florence Nightingale Teacher's Activity Book

Introduction

Some children will have personal experience of hospital wards and others will have visited relatives, or perhaps a newly born baby. Many will probably have seen hospitals in television dramas.

This E Big Book sets out to engage pupils in Years 1 and 2 in finding out about Florence Nightingale and her impact on the development of hospital care. In doing so, they will explore how and why she was, and is still, famous.

Aims of the book

1. To promote children's developing sense of chronology
2. To help children recognise that there are similarities and differences between aspects of life in the past and present
3. To enable children to develop conclusions of their own through careful study of a range of pictorial material
4. To provide a basis for opportunities to develop children's literacy skills

How to use the E Big Book

This resource meets some of the breadth of study requirements of National Curriculum History, particularly:

- the way of life of people in the more distant past
- the life of a significant woman drawn from the history of Britain.

It provides scope to develop children's ability to:

- place events and objects in chronological order
- use common words and phrases relating to the passage of time (e.g. before, after, then, now)
- recognise why people did things, why events happened and what happened as a result
- identify differences between ways of life at different times
- find out about the past from an appropriate range of sources of information, and ask and answer questions about the past
- select from their knowledge of history tend communicate it in a variety of ways (e.g. talking, writing).

At first, teachers m photographs witho observe them closely.

All photographs can be printed separately with margins suitable for children to label key features to show their knowledge and understanding. Questions could also be posed for other children to answer by looking carefully at the photograph and/or drawing on their wider knowledge.

There are three audio buttons. Click on **Read aloud** for Magic Grandad reading the main text. The **Hear more** buttons provide more material on each theme, often drawing children's attention to features of the photographs by raising questions. Clicking on the **Sound button** results in a nurse talking about healthcare today.

Opportunities to develop literacy skills

The material in this E Big Book provides considerable scope to contribute to children's growing literacy skills. Each spread presents opportunities for careful observation of the photographs and subsequent discussion, promoting vital speaking and listening skills. The modelling of skills by the teacher will be helpful, with children expected to develop their ideas orally in an ordered and engaging manner and to listen actively and ask relevant questions. Ordering ideas and practising particular sentence structures will make a valuable contribution to the development of writing.

The nature and extent of the contribution made by this book will vary with the age and stage of development of the children. The teacher is the best judge of how to use this resource. Opportunities for writing might include:

- shared and/or individual writing of captions for particular photographs
- writing extended captions, which are likely to be linked with better historical understanding
- writing simple questions that could be answered from the text
- contributing to a class book about Florence Nightingale
- compiling a class dictionary of words connected with Florence's life

- organising information about hospital wards today and in the mid-nineteenth century into a simple chart or table. This will support/consolidate children's understanding of similarities and differences
- making simple notes to support children's own subsequent writing
- writing a simple account of events in Florence's life
- writing an explanatory account of the ways in which Florence helped to improve hospitals.

There is also scope for:

- reinforcing recognition of full stops and capital letters
- covering words and inviting children to predict, based on preceding words in the sentence
- using and consolidating the term 'sentence'
- developing understanding that a non-fiction text such as this can be read in sections to find information needed, rather than from start to finish
- using the contents page
- developing phonological awareness, spelling and vocabulary throughout, as required.

Questions in the E Big Book

1. Why did Florence Nightingale become famous and how did she help to improve hospitals?
2. What were hospitals like one hundred and fifty years ago?
3. What was Florence's childhood like?
4. Where did the Nightingales visit and how did they travel?
5. How did Florence show she really wanted to be a nurse?
6. What were hospitals like in the Crimea and how did Florence help?
7. How did Mary Seacole help the soldiers?
8. How did Florence use her fame to help people?
9. How did Florence still help people even when she was ill?
10. What were Florence's main achievements?

Hospitals today and long ago

Use the picture of the children's ward to assist in prompting children to identify features of a hospital ward today. Friendly nurses and doctors, proper beds and regular meals will doubtless be among the items.

Things were very different one hundred and fifty years ago and it is important to establish with children what things were like before changes took place. Lack of proper nurses, the poor state of patients, dark and dirty buildings and lack of appropriate beds are likely to be among the features discussed.

Hear more

When I visited my grandson in hospital, it was a cheerful place with lots of doctors and nurses. Hospitals one hundred and fifty years ago were very different. Can you spot some reasons why it was impossible to keep wards clean?

Activity sheet 1 — AS 1

Ask children to add one or more sentences to show some differences between hospitals today and one hundred and fifty years ago.

Florence's childhood

Explore with children where they have been on holiday and for how long. Some will almost certainly have been abroad for one or two weeks. If you are very lucky, someone may have been to Florence in Italy! Point out that, when Florence was young, wealthy people went on the Grand Tour. This involved visiting key cultural sites in Europe and often took many months. William Nightingale and his new wife Frances were away for two years on their honeymoon, and both Florence and her older sister Parthenope were born during this period.

When in Britain, the Nightingales divided their time between their two homes. Both houses were large by modern standards, although Embley Park was the largest. How do children think that the very long holidays and the two houses might have affected the two sisters' education? In fact, Florence and Parthenope did not go to school. Like many wealthy girls of the time, they were educated at home. They were luckier than most, for William Nightingale firmly believed that girls should be properly educated. Most wealthy fathers thought it was enough that their daughters should learn how to run a household.

Hear more

Florence was quite lucky as her parents had two houses! The chimneys at Embley Park give us some clues about how many rooms there might have been. Can you count them?

Activity sheet 2 — AS 2
Ask children to write about the Nightingales' two houses and to think about which one Florence might have preferred.

Her travels

Have any of the children been on holiday to any of the countries that the Nightingales visited? How did they travel there? It will not have been in a carriage like the one seen here! Ask children to look closely at the picture. What do they think it might have been like to travel in such a vehicle? It was certainly very slow, which contributed to the amount of time taken for the Grand Tour. What souvenirs have children brought back from their holidays? How do they compare with Florence's? Florence's pet owl was called Athena because Florence found her in Athens. Athena was Florence's pet for some years.

Hear more

Florence's family travelled a lot. Her sister, Parthenope, was named after the Greek word for another Italian city: Naples. Florence liked to bring things home to help her remember her travels. Can you spot the perfume she brought back from Italy? What do people in your class bring back from their holidays?

Activity sheet 3 — AS 3
Children can show their knowledge and understanding by writing about the family's travels when Florence was young.

Her interest in nursing

Can children remember anything from Florence's childhood that might provide a clue to her interest in nursing? Revisiting 'Florence's childhood' will remind them. Florence's parents were very unhappy with her wish to become a nurse. In those days, this was not the career for a rich young woman. But Florence was very determined – a characteristic that stood in her good stead for much of her life. Ask the children to look at the drawing room of Embley Park. This gives some idea of how grand the house was. Can they spot the huge fireplace? Notice the elaborate clothes of wealthy ladies.

It was Florence's trip to Germany that gave her the opportunity for training. Ask children to look at the picture of the children's ward. Can they spot the different kinds of beds and the nurses? Children may be surprised that Florence would take on a job in London with no pay. This reflects both her commitment and her wealthy background, as her father could give her enough money (£500 per year – a substantial sum at that time) to live on.

Hear more

Although her parents were against the idea, Florence wanted to become a nurse. Can you find Florence's signature on her letter accepting a job in a hospital in London? Look carefully to see if you can find out when she wrote this letter.

Activity sheet 4 — AS 4
Children decide which of the statements Florence might have made.

The Crimean War

There is no real need to discuss the reasons for the Crimean War. Children might be impressed by the size of the Scutari hospital, but it was not built as a hospital. It was a soldiers' barracks that the British decided to use for this purpose.

Why do children think conditions in the hospital were so bad? It was partly sheer weight of numbers but also the lack of sufficient care on the wards. In addition, germs had not yet been discovered, so the true significance of the filthy conditions was not apparent. At first, the doctors and army officers, who were all men, were hostile and contemptuous of what the women might achieve. But Florence and her 38 nurses worked very hard to improve the cleanliness of the bedding and the quality of the food. This did not have much effect on the number of deaths. These only started to fall when inspectors sent out from London found and removed a dead horse in the water supply and cleared the drains.

Florence's 'lady with the lamp' soubriquet arose later, greatly boosted by a poem by Longfellow. Soldiers called her 'lady in chief'. However, the 'lamp' became famous and figured prominently in many drawings of her at Scutari by artists who had never been there. What the lamp was actually like is seen in the picture. Compare this with the elaborate lamps shown in other books.

Ask children to look carefully at the picture of Florence at Scutari. What is she doing? Why were the beds were so close together? Do the children think the artist had been there?

Hear more

The hospital at Scutari looks impressive on the outside but inside it was damp and dirty. Notice how dark it is in the picture of Florence in one of the wards. Can you spot another wounded soldier being carried in? It would have been hard work to keep this ward clean.

Activity sheet 5 — AS 5
Ask children to add some sentences about Florence's work at Scutari.

Mary Seacole

Mary Seacole is less well known than Florence Nightingale and has only featured significantly in books in the last twenty years or so. Mary was 15 years older than Florence and born in Jamaica. She was the daughter of a Jamaican woman and a Scottish army officer. She was an expert in herbal remedies and nursed victims of disease in Panama and Jamaica. Although keen to offer her services in Britain when the Crimean War broke out, Mary was rejected by the government. She wondered later whether it was due to her colour. She certainly did not fit the mould of Florence Nightingale – a woman from a wealthy background who would be in charge – and she was too skilled just to clean wards.

Can the children suggest any evidence of Mary being famous at the time? Her medal from Queen Victoria is perhaps the best. But why is she less well known than Florence? We know less about her due to her humbler origins in the West Indies. She also lacked the wealthy family and friends who helped Florence both before and after the war.

Hear more

Mary Seacole helped the soldiers too. Mary's gravestone tells us a little about her. Where did she come from and where else did she help the sick and wounded? Can you find these places on a map or a globe?

Activity sheet 6 — AS 6
Ask children to show their understanding of the differences between Florence and Mary by matching the statements to the correct person.

Florence's fame

What kind of people are famous today? What are the trappings of fame? Children will provide examples that include football and pop stars, and may suggest expensive cars and clothes, huge houses, TV appearances and travel to exotic locations. What were the trappings of fame for Florence and how were they similar and different? Importantly, Florence was uncomfortable with her fame and sought to put it to good use, establishing the nursing school at St Thomas' Hospital in 1860.

Hear more

Can you find some of the evidence that Florence became famous? She did not like being well known, but she wanted to make sure that there were properly trained nurses in hospitals in Britain. Can you see the famous building behind St Thomas' Hospital in London?

Activity sheet 7 — AS 7
Children can show their understanding of the impact of Florence's fame by adding sentences to explain each picture.

Her later years

Florence was often ill after her experiences in the Crimea and frequently bedridden. But she worked hard from her house at 10 South Street, Mayfair, with the support of her friends and family. The houses in South Street were demolished in the 1920s, but the drawing shown here gives a good idea of what a well-to-do city street in late Victorian times looked like.

If the house has been demolished, ask children if they can think where the photograph of the drawing room has come from. It is, in fact, of a reconstruction at the Florence Nightingale Museum in London. We can often get a good idea of what rooms were like in the past from well-researched museum reconstructions such as this. Ask children what the large number of nurses attending the memorial service tells us about their opinion of Florence.

| Hear more |

Although she was often ill, Florence worked hard to improve hospitals. She often wrote letters giving advice or making suggestions. Can you see her writing desk in the colour photograph? Look at the photo of nurses going to Florence's memorial service after she died. How are they different from the nurses you saw before Florence became famous?

Activity sheet 8 — AS 8

Ask children to choose which statements might have been made by someone attending Florence's memorial service. Some could go on to write more to show how highly regarded she was by nurses at the time of her death.

What Florence achieved

Can children pick out the various health professionals in the photographs? Do they or their family and friends have experience of the support of any of these? In various ways, these services were started on their way by Florence Nightingale.

| Hear more |

King Edward VII gave Florence the Order of Merit to recognise what she had done. Can you spot the clue that this was a royal medal? See if you can work out from the photographs which groups of people are still benefiting from the results of Florence's work today.

Activity sheet 9 — AS 9

As an alternative to the approach on the activity sheet, copy and cut out the pictures. Then ask children to sort the pictures into the correct sequence and glue them onto a sheet of paper. They could then write a sentence for each. Some could use the pictures to help them write an account of key events in Florence's life.

AS 1 Hospitals today and long ago

Name _____ Date _____

What were hospitals like one hundred and fifty years ago and what are they like today?

Today

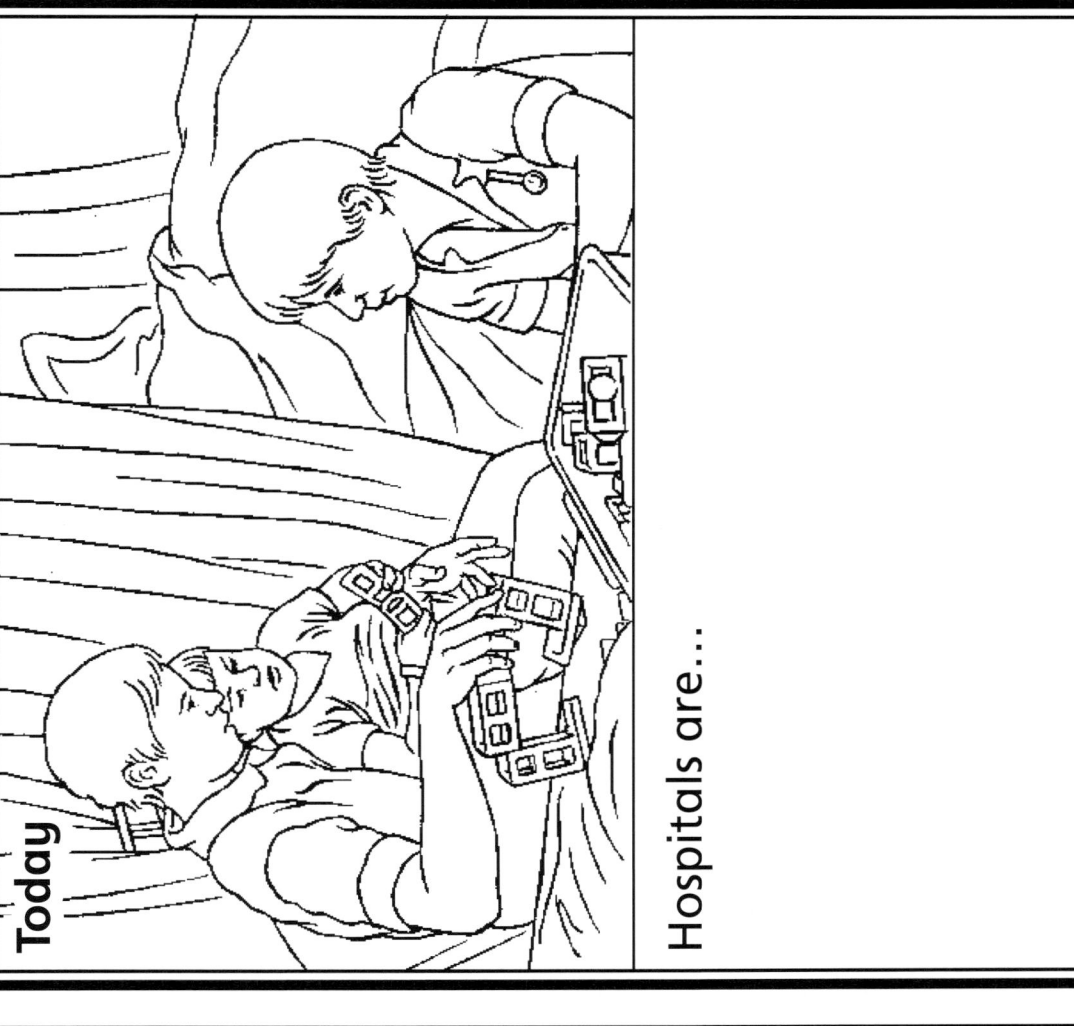

Hospitals are…

One hundred and fifty years ago

Hospitals were…

Some words to use: cheerful, clean, dirty, friendly, nurses, trained

BBC Active Magic Grandad: Florence Nightingale

AS 2 Florence's childhood

Name _____ Date _____

Write about each of Florence's childhood homes.

The Nightingales lived…

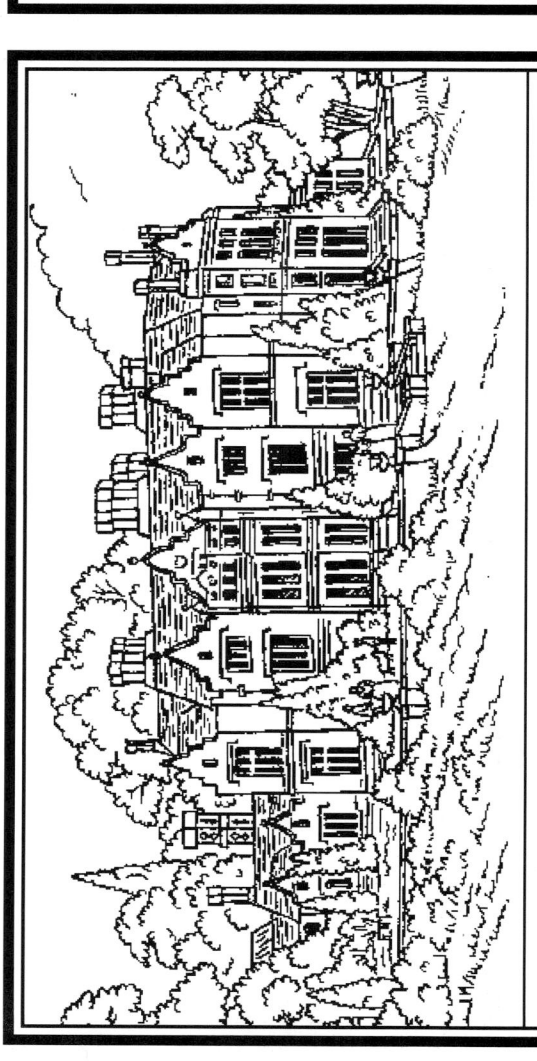

The Nightingales lived…

Which house do you think Florence liked living in most and why?

Some words to use: Lea Hurst, Embley Park, summer, winter, mansion, Derbyshire, Hampshire

BBC Active *Magic Grandad: Florence Nightingale*

AS 3 Her travels

Name _____ Date _____

Describe Florence's family holidays.

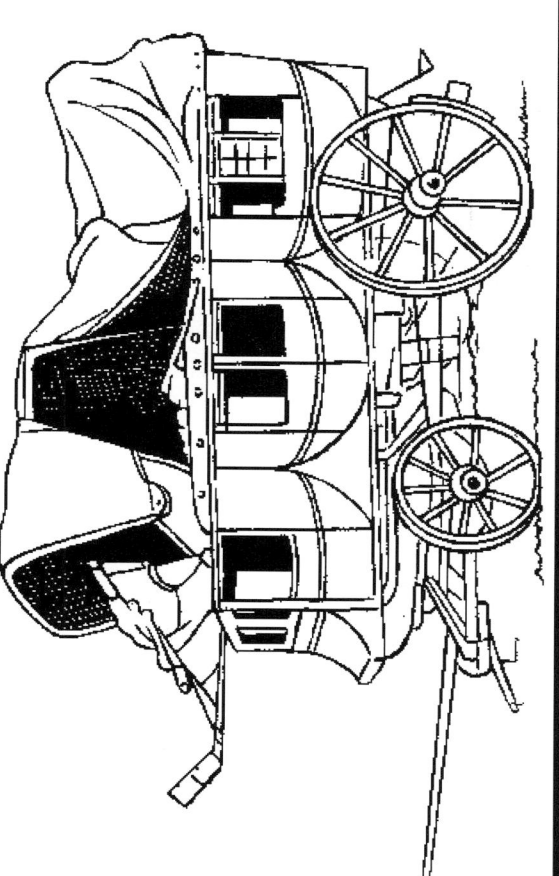

The Nightingales went...

They vistited...

Travelling was...

Some words to use: carriage, holidays, long, France, Italy, Switzerland, Greece, Germany, Egypt, slow, horses, difficult, bumpy, pulled

BBC Active *Magic Grandad: Florence Nightingale*

AS 4 Her interest in nursing

Which of these statements might Florence have said?

- Please let me be a nurse. ☐
- Hospitals are not the place for a young lady! ☐
- I want to be a nurse. ☐
- I want to help people who are not as lucky as me. ☐

AS 5 The Crimean War

Name _____ Date _____

Describe what Florence did to help the soldiers during the Crimean War.

Florence made sure…

She also…

The soldiers…

Some words to use: wards, clean, clothes, bedding, grateful, food, lady-in-chief

BBC Active Magic Grandad: Florence Nightingale

AS 6 Mary Seacole

Name _____ Date _____

Who would have said the following statements?
Write the numbers under the correct picture.

1. I was born in Italy.
2. I was born in Jamaica.
3. The government asked me to help.
4. The government did not want me to help.
5. The soldiers called me 'lady-in-chief'.
6. The soldiers called me 'Mother Seacole'.

BBC Active Magic Grandad: Florence Nightingale

AS 7 Florence's fame

Name _____ Date _____

Write about each picture below.

Some words to use: pottery doll, money, training, famous, nurses, nursing school, poster

BBC Active *Magic Grandad: Florence Nightingale*

AS 8 Her later years

Name _____ Date _____

Which statements are true or false? Tick or cross to the correct box to show your answer.

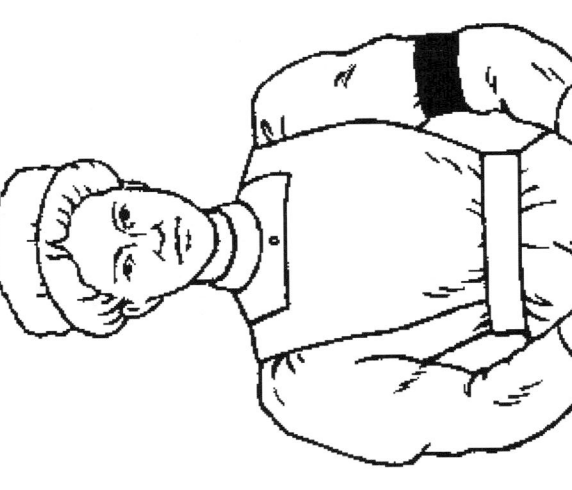

I am going to the memorial service for Florence Nightingale because:	✓	✗
She helped soldiers in the Crimean War.		
She set up a school in London to train nurses.		
She gave advice about new hospitals and nursing schools.		
She loved being famous.		

Imagine you are a nurse at the memorial service. Explain to a friend why you have come. What would you say?

AS 9 What Florence achieved

Name _____ Date _____

These drawings show the different stages of Florence Nightingale's life. Put them in the correct order by giving each a number from 1 to 6.

The Order of Merit

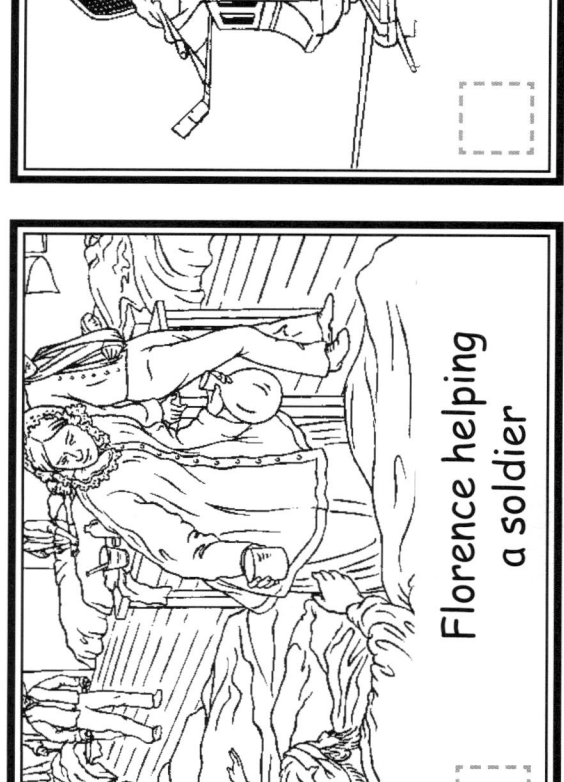
The carriage

Florence, Italy

Florence helping a soldier

Kaiserswerth ward

Florence surrounded by nurses

BBC Active *Magic Grandad: Florence Nightingale*

Further resources

For teachers

Hugh Small, *Florence Nightingale, Avenging Angel* (Constable, 1998)

Richard Tames, *Florence Nightingale* (Franklin Watts, 1989)

For children

Jane Shuter, *Florence Nightingale* (Heinemann, 2001)

Nina Morgan, *Florence Nightingale* (Hodder Wayland Life Stories, 1999)

Stewart Ross, *Don't Say No to Flo: the Story of Florence Nightingale*, Stories from History series (Hodder Wayland, 2002)

Rebecca Vickers, *Florence Nightingale* (Heinemann, 2002)

Internet

The Florence Nightingale Museum in London has a helpful website for teachers:

www.florence-nightingale.co.uk

Country Joe McDonald's website has interesting material for teachers:

www.countryjoe.com/nightingale

The Mary Seacole Centre for Nursing Practice has a useful website:

www.maryseacole.com

Blacknet has a developing area on black history:

www.blacknet.co.uk/history/Mary.html

The Black History Month website includes useful pages on Mary:

www.black-history-month.co.uk/articles/legacy_mary_seacole.html

Places to visit

The Florence Nightingale Museum is a popular destination for schools in London. There are specially prepared materials to support visits by children of varying ages. Schools from further afield will find it well worth contacting the museum for postcards, books and other items.

The Florence Nightingale Museum
2 Lambeth Palace Road
London
SE1 7EW

(tel: 020 7620 0374)